The Emperor's Cool Clothes

ADAPTED AND
ILLUSTRATED BY
**LEE
HARPER**

MARSHALL CAVENDISH CHILDREN

Paul

The Emperor

Radford

Text and illustrations copyright © 2011 by Lee Harper

Marshall Cavendish Corporation

99 White Plains Road

Tarrytown, NY 10591

www.marshallcavendish.us/kids

Library of Congress Cataloging-in-Publication Data

Harper, Lee

The Emperor's cool clothes / adapted and illustrated by Lee Harper.
— 1st ed.

p. cm.

Summary: Two rascally weavers convince the emperor they are making clothing that will make him look "cool" and will let him know who else is "cool," as well, but when he wears them during the Royal Parade, a child cries out that the emperor has nothing on. Includes author's note about the story's origins.

ISBN 978-0-7614-5948-4 (hardcover) ISBN 978-0-7614-5996-5 (ebook)

[1. Fairy tales.] I. Andersen, H. C. (Hans Christian), 1805-1875.

Kejserens nye klaeder. II. Title.

PZ8.H237Emp 2011 [E]—dc22 2010024234

The illustrations are rendered in watercolor and pencil on 140 pound Arches hot press watercolor paper.

Editor: Robin Benjamin

Printed in China (E)

First edition

10 9 8 7 6 5 4 3 2 1

Marshall Cavendish Children

Frostbite   Tusks

A special thanks to my editor, Robin Benjamin, whose "cool" idea this was in the first place

AUTHOR'S NOTE

The Emperor's New Clothes was written by the Danish author Hans Christian Andersen and first published in 1837. Similar tales have been written in many cultures around the world, with each version being a little different, depending on where and when it was written. Hans Christian Andersen's version was set in Denmark and meant to be a satirical story about the hypocrisy and snobbery he saw in high society, and also about having the courage to tell the truth.

The theme is as relevant today as ever. Vanity can make people go to great extremes to impress others. And it can make them look downright silly. I've set my story in an imaginary kingdom where emperor penguins, walruses, albatross, seals, and polar bears all live—and shop—together.   —*Lee Harper*

There once lived an emperor....

When he was young, the other kids made fun of him:

After he became emperor, he grew obsessed with looking *totally cool*.
And how could he achieve that?

The emperor had a different outfit for every hour of every day.

But he was never able to achieve total coolness.

He searched all the shops in town, but nothing seemed cool enough.

Then he found a store he'd never seen before.

"Hello, I'm Paul Rogue, and this is my brother, Radford. Our clothes are made with a special formula that makes them invisible to anyone who's not totally cool like you."

"So you'll always know who's cool, and who isn't," added Radford.

The emperor handed over his platinum card.

The two Rogues told the emperor they'd get right to work buying gold thread and silk to weave his new clothes.

But they didn't.

They just shopped online for themselves: yachts, vacation houses, jewelry, and fancy clothes.

The next day, the emperor decided to send someone to check on his new clothes.

It needs to be someone cool enough to see them, he thought. *Hmmmm. . . .*

He decided on Frostbite, his Councillor of Cool.

The Rogues described the colors and patterns.

Frostbite couldn't see the clothes, but he didn't want anyone to know.

"What do you think?" asked Paul.

"They're cool as a blizzard!" said Frostbite. "I'll tell the emperor."

With the emperor's money, the Rogues bought more and more stuff for themselves. . . .

After a few more days, the emperor decided to send Tusks, his Chancellor of Chill, to see how the weaving was coming along.

"What do you think?" asked Paul.
Tusks couldn't see the clothes, either, but he said,
"They're cool as an Arctic breeze! I'll tell the emperor."

Soon the emperor's cool clothes were the talk of the town.
The emperor decided he had to see them for himself.

He and his top advisors went to visit the shop.

They stared at the empty loom. . . .

"Well, do you like them?" asked Tusks.

"Don't you just love them, Emps?" asked Frostbite.

Uh-oh, thought the emperor. *If I can't see the clothes, maybe I'm not cool?*

Finally, the emperor declared:

The Rogues pretended to work all night. They set up spotlights so everyone could see how busy they were. They pretended to take the material down from the loom.

They used needles without thread. They swung scissors in the air.
And in the morning they announced: "The clothes are ready!"

The Rogues arrived at the palace with a big box and pretended to pull out the new clothes while the emperor took off his old ones.

"See the pants!" said Radford.

"Here's the robe," said Paul, "woven with silk so light, you'll think you're wearing nothing at all!"

The Rogues pretended to put each new garment on the emperor.

"Wow, they fit perfectly! What patterns! What colors! You look *totally cool*!" gushed Frostbite and Tusks.

It was time for the parade to begin. Tusks and Frostbite pretended to hold the emperor's train in the air. No one in the crowd would admit that they could see nothing. Everyone said, "What patterns! What colors! He looks *totally cool*!"

At last, a little girl cried out . . .

"BUT HE HAS NOTHING ON!"

Soon everyone agreed that—in fact—the emperor was parading down the street completely naked!

What can I do? thought the emperor. *I can't stop now.*

And so, he paraded through the streets in the world's coolest clothes, which did not exist at all.